STORIES FROM A KERRY FIRESIDE

STORIES FROM A KERRY FIRESIDE

JOHN B. KEANE

THE MERCIER PRESS
DUBLIN and CORK

The Mercier Press Limited
4, Bridge Street, Cork
25 Lower Abbey Street, Dublin 1

ISBN 0 85342 621 X

The author and publisher wish to acknowledge that these stories were previously published in *The Limerick Leader, The Evening Herald,* Radio Éireann and BBC.

Printed by Litho Press Co., Midleton, Co. Cork.

CONTENTS

To Eileen and Derry

1 Shy Singers

The last American wake which I attended was held to mourn the departure of a far-out cousin. There was a half tierce of porter perched on a trestle near the doorway and whenever a man wanted a fresh drink all he had to do was turn on the tap. In the 'Room' there was stronger drink such as whiskey, brandy and poitín. There was no word of vodka in those days and the most an average female would indulge in was a tint or two of sherry on the grounds that anything stronger might go to her head.

There had been singing and dancing all night and it was well into the morning when I heard a faint and distant voice rendering that fine old ballad *The Yorkshire Pigs:*

> From Glounshanoon to Glashnanoon and from Brasna to Meengwee
> There'll be slips and stores from well-bred boars to fill the whole country.
> If you go to a dance, a wake or a prance for to practise your reels and jigs
> The ladies can't stay. They must hasten away for to fatten the Yorkshire Pigs.

From time to time there were words of encouragement from the listeners but nowhere could I see the person who was singing. The voice seemed to come from the open doorway so I finished my mug of porter, filled a fresh one and made for the door where I beheld the singer. He was a tall, gangly, pale-faced fellow in his forties. He stood with his back to the wall of the house, head erect, poll pressed to the cold plaster. He sang with his eyes partly shut but not so shut as not to see me when I appeared in the doorway. Immediately he turned his head in the opposite direction and sang sideways through an open window. When he finished, to considerable applause, he ran off behind a neighbouring hayshed and wasn't seen for the remainder of the night. Here was a shy singer, a man who could not bear to be watched while he sang or applauded when his contribution was over. His likes were indigenous enough to the countryside but townspeople tended to laugh at him. Alas it was the laughter of misunderstanding for these men had a most significant contribution to make to the cultural life of the countryside. During the Stations they would sing from outside the house through an open window or, if the weather was too cold, from a room adjacent to the one where the priests were eating. This was the equivalent of what people in the cities call background music. It never intruded in the conversation and the source of the song was never seen. No string quartet could match this delightful arrangement for sheer subtlety. Singing through doors and windows, however, was only the half of it. There were bolder performers who remained within the precincts of the area where the function, be it wake, Station, wren-dance or ordinary hooley, was being held.

These, of course, were basically shy to begin with and for one reason or another had graduated indoors over the years and had drifted down phase by phase from the 'Room' of their own accord. The great majority of this category would tender their renditions with their faces to the wall or indeed to the windows or door, in fact towards anywhere so long as their backs were turned to their audiences. There were, of course, variations. Some would sit in the corner near the hearth and face the hob. Then at the tops of their voices they would sing up the chimney. Long, lonesome songs were a distinct failure in this respect as most of the sound was carried aloft by the draught and dispersed without purpose in the night air outside. A short snappy song such as the *Ballygologue Brigade* or the *Geese in the Bog* stood a far better chance of success than say for instance *The Shores of Amerikay* or that awful tragic masterpiece *The Burnt Pup*. Interest was quickly lost if the words or melody were inclined to drag. The ideal choice was, of course, *The Ballygologue Brigade,* one of the few surviving songs about the Kerry Militia which went something like this:

> In all my life a soldier I was never drilled but once
> In the Kerry Militia Barracks under Corporal Dinny Bunce.
> He said you broken soldier and he tapped me on the poll
> I'll have your name your leg is lame knocked off the Munster Roll.
> Then off to hospital I was sent and on a hammock laid
> Because I couldn't keep up the step with the Ballygologue Brigade.

9

The best shy singer I ever heard was a servant boy whose name was Devane. His method was to go under the table and stay there for the duration of the night with his own bucket of porter and a mug. He crawled out only when nature called. Whenever his services were required someone knocked upon the table with the mallet which was used for˙ tapping the porter barrels and Devane would deliver the goods without the usual preamble of threatening or coaxing. If anybody peeped under the table while he was singing he would stop dead or if he was drunk he might draw a swipe of a fist or of the bucket if it was empty at the curious party. Like all worthwhile artists he was temperamental and over-emotional and it was extremely difficult to start him off again after a deliberate interruption. He had no objection to people sitting on the table as long as they did not swing their legs. When his bucket was empty he banged it noisily on the floor and it was always re-filled immediately lest he overturn the table and depart in a huff.

Common too was another shy variety who used implements and utensils to conceal themselves from a curious public. The favourite implements were pot-covers, griddles or the covers of tea-chests. These were held in front of the face while the song was being sung. Often in the case of an elderly person or a very young person the implement would be held by one or more assistants. These assistants dare not look upon the visage of the singer and only dour, sober, reliable men were entrusted with this particular job. Another favourite utensil was a bucket down over a man's head until it reached his chin. This way he could not see the faces of his audience nor could they see his.

Thus protected he sang away to his heart's content. Another valid reason why certain singers preferred to hide themselves was that there might be a certain member of the audience who had an off-putting effect on them. It might be a lesser singer filled with jealousy or the trustee of an old family feud. These were unsympathetic forces and a grimace or grin from this direction could easily put an artist off. Under the bucket there was no danger of such a thing happening. However, there was a catch. The bucket was regarded as an aid in that it enriched poor voices and enlarged small ones. It was acceptable but its users were not regarded in the same class as the man who sang down from the 'Room' or sideways through an open window. Looking back now over the years I recall that shy singers far outnumbered natural or normal singers. These latter were somewhat suspect and were believed to have hard necks. How else could they stand unabashed in front of their neighbours and perform as if it were the commonest thing in the world? There was more thought of the bashful entertainer who was too shy or too gentlemanly to look his fellows in the face while he regaled them with his noblest efforts.

Until quite recently I was convinced that shy singers of the kinds I have mentioned were extinct in the countryside. I was delighted to be proved wrong. A group of us were on our way from a funeral when one of our party suggested we stop at a rustic hostelry for the dual purpose of breaking our journey and tossing back a measure or two to the memory of the faithful departed. The pub was crowded with other mourners and after a while there was a lively sing-song in progress. It was late in the night when I heard that unforgettable sound. The boss of the house had called upon a youth called Jackeen to sing a song. I could see that the lad was reluctant to oblige even when we clamoured for a contribution. Then impetuously the poor fellow jumped up and whispered some words into the ear of the proprietor. The proprietor nodded and smiled and patted the lad on the back after which he went quickly out of doors only to return immediately with an empty enamel bucket over his head. Then he sang as only your shy singer can, with all his strength and with all his heart:

> So here's to the man who lives while he can and success to the man who digs,
> May we all live to see oul' Ireland free and to hell with the Yorkshire Pigs.

2 The Stacks Mountains

Last week I revisited the Stacks mountains where I was reared and countrified. I arrived in a new car but I had hardly set foot in the townland I knew as a boy when I was reminded of my first visit and my departure. I came in a creamery lorry and I departed aboard Jumpin' Hanlon's pony-drawn fishcart. Jumpin' who had a fish shop a few doors down the street from my father's house in Listowel would come in September with a load of fresh mackerel. His full name was James Jumpin' Alive O'Hanlon. He acquired his nickname from the way he responded when asked if his fish were fresh.

'Man dear,' he would say, 'they're jumpin' alive.'

Then he would choose an outstanding specimen and hold it in his hands in such a way that it seemed to jump from his grasp of its own accord.

Catch that fish,' he would call out, 'catch that fish in God's name don't let it go home to Caherciveen.'

That would be the tatarara as he went on all fours to seize the mackerel which, as soon as he recovered it, would jump out of his hand again until finally he was obliged to tap it on the head with his knuckles to make sure it didn't return to that wild part of the Atlantic from whence at first it came.

I returned every year to the Stacks mountains for those long summer holidays until I reached the age of fifteen. I still frequently return to the warm, secure home where I was reared when Hitler was shrieking his head off in Berlin and innocent Irishmen were dying in distant places like Tobruk and Alamein, men from the Stacks at that, long before their time in useless carnage, carefree boys whose only weapons until that time were the hayfork and the turf-slean who wanted only the right to work and play and find a place at the table.

I have already written a short book about the matchmaker Dan Paddy Andy O'Sullivan but if his name crops up now and again don't hold it against me. Dan was to the Stacks mountains what bark is to the tree. Any *cursíos* about the Stacks mountains would be incomplete without Dan Paddy Andy. Dan would, no doubt, have been the most famous name in the area. The wealthiest is a man in England who doesn't like having his name mentioned.

The Second World War was the best time to be in the Stacks mountains. There was no man nor boy who didn't have a shilling in his pocket. There was an insatiable demand for turf and Lyreacrompane was the home of it. Man, woman and child took to the bogs across the summers and for the first time in the history of that much abused, much deprived community every person who wasn't disabled or sick had a pound or two to spare.

Buyers would come from Tralee, Castleisland, Abbeyfeale and Listowel on the look-out for likely roadside ricks to fill the wagons waiting at the railway depots in the aforementioned towns. Those who journeyed to the towns with horse, ass, mule and pony rails were often met a mile outside by buyers with outstanding orders to fill. In addition the Kerry County

Council initiated a turf-cutting campaign in order to supply cheap fuel to the many institutions under its care. This even ensured jobs for townies if they wanted them.

In the Stacks there were no villages but there were several shops such as Lyre Post Office, Doran's, Nolan's and McElligott's and, of course, there was Dan Paddy Andy O'Sullivan's famous dance hall at the crossroads of Renagown. There were three or four visiting butchers and fishmongers and occasional travelling salesmen, mostly Pakistani with huge trunks of wispy undergarments, scarves and frocks perched precariously on the carriers, of ancient bicycles. I remember two of these quite well.

There was 'Likey Nicey Tie' and 'Likey Nicey Knickeys'. The latter often indicated that he was prepared to exchange his wares for the favours of the country ladies. As far as I know he never did any business in this fashion. In our youthful ignorance we would stalk them as far as the Cross of Renagown shouting 'Likey Nicey Tie, Likey Nicey Knickeys' and most heinous of all 'Likey Pig's Bum'.

We had been informed by hobside know-alls that these coloured salesmen would be damned if they ate any kind of pig's meat but doubly damned if it was the rear of a pig. We didn't know any better. We were young and backward and wouldn't know prejudice from the prod of a thorn.

3 An Ear for Speech

In the pub the other night I decided to opt out of the conversation. Very often a man with a good ear for speech can be nobly entertained if he is prepared to sit quietly and contemplate the ramblings and musings of his fellows. Davy Gunn the *bodhrán*-maker was making a point.

'If I had enough goats,' Davy said as I sipped my drink in a quiet corner of the bar, 'I'd make pucks of money but don't ask me to buy no bawnie. I made *bodhráns* of bawnie skins and they made no battle at all God help us.' A bawnie, of course, is a white goat or white cow. 'The best place for goats I ever came across,' Davy confided, 'is Croagh in the County Limerick. 'Tis there the good land is.'

Apparently the Croagh goats have better bones and are much larger in size. They have sleeker, more consistent hides which provide an excellent tone when tanned.

'It isn't,' said Davy, 'but all goats are choosy pickers and only eat the best like one of ourselves would go for the lean meat or the fillet.'

Listening was a man from the townland of Kilbaha which is due north of Listowel. 'Your goat,' said he, 'if you had a goat won't eat musty hay. He'll eat your galluses first.'

'Yes,' Davy Gunn quickly agreed, 'and if you were to make a stack of four and forty wynds of hay and let

16

you say to yourself that it was poor quality except one wynd where the harvest was light and dried well, be sure your goat will find that wynd no matter in what corner of the rick 'tis stuck.'

'So would a donkey,' the Kilbaha man put in.

'So he would,' said Davy, 'for with all their breeding your Friesian and Whitehead will eat direct till he comes to the good cock by accident, not saying he'll turn his back on it when he comes to it for he'll fly in-to it like 'twas the clover of June.'

'Oh the clover of June,' repeated the Kilbaha man savouring the phrase with the dedicated intonation it deserved. 'The clover of June to be sure.'

'And where are you leaving your deer?' asked a man from Rathea to the south of Listowel.

'Your deer don't come down town no more,' Davy reminded him, 'too busy for him down below.'

'Faith indeed I often eat venison,' put in a Killarney man. 'I ate it in the bochtawn thirties when I couldn't grind the free beef.'

'Oh indeed there was wan time,' said the Kilbaha man, 'and we'd eat frostnails after Dev had the row with England and the calves was choking the eyes of the bridges and our backsides coming out through our trousers and we not having the price of a Woodbine.'

'Well they're not choking them now,' said Davy Gunn, 'and maybe 'tis how Dev's policy has paid off in the long run.'

'A very long run you might say,' from the Kilbaha man.

Sensing an all-out political argument the astute Rathea man steered the conversation towards the open sea.

'They were hard times,' the Rathea man reminded all and sundry of the several who stood in the same clump at the counter. Some shook their heads as they recalled the period. It was a time that most would prefer to forget. Indeed it was a shameful time for some because of the grinding poverty.

'There is trouble now,' said Davy Gunn, 'because nearly everyone has money and the few that hasn't are the odd ones out. Long 'go no one had money and we were all in the same boat. That's why you had no trouble like you have today. The poverty was spread more even.'

'Long 'go ladies went to England and turned into streetwalkers,' said the Kilbaha man. 'What they often gave away here for a packet of Woodbines they'd get a ten shilling note for over and that was money in them days.'

There was a general murmur of agreement with these findings.

'In them days,' said Davy Gunn, 'you'd get two good calves for ten bob.'

Then came the ultimate story in poverty. It was told by a sallow man who had made no contribution to the conversation up to this. The time was 1933. It was a misty evening in the dockland of a well-known Irish port. It was also winter-time and not even the seagulls mewed in the desolate skies. A lone sailor trudged aimlessly back to his ship. Gradually a female shape emerged from the mist and accosted him. He dismissed her with a deprecatory wave of his hand but she persisted. Who knows but she had a baby to feed or a workless man to support.

'Go away girl,' said he, 'all I have to my name is

one threepenny bit.'

'That's alright,' said the lady of easy virtue, 'I have change for it.'

At this stage unfortunately I had to leave but there should have been a small boy with a recording machine employed to capture the remaining conversation. There was a time when the Folklore Commission thought 't worth its while to gather the folk tales of the countryside but is not the folk speech just as important? It will not be the same in ten years' time. It will have gone altogether in fifty years' time and with it the colour, whimsy, uniqueness of expression and all the other flourishes which gave to the country and to the world so many fine poems and ballads in such an unusual form. I wonder how many people are really aware of the fact that a distinct way of speech is dying and is about to be no more.

4 Scratchers I Have Known

Some years ago I wrote a short essay on the subject of scratching. Time now to have a closer look at this fascinating subject. At Mass last Sunday I beheld in front of me a youth who scratched himself from stem to stern during the entire length of the sacred proceedings. Here indeed was a genuine phenomenon.

Here was the first bout of comprehensive scratching practised in the public eye for a generation. When I was a youngster everybody scratched themselves. There were varying reasons. D.D.T. had not yet made its appearance and colonies of half-starved fleas were as common as freckles on the heads and trunks of the unwashed, the unkempt and the unfumigated. Even those who fervently believed that cleanliness was next to Godliness were not without lengthy visits from itinerant fleas.

There were local names for these blood-thirsty vagrants. Some called them 'boodies' while others simply labelled them 'nits'. Almost every mother in the country would, on Saturday night, institute an exhaustive search with fine tooth combs for these insignificant terrors. Only boodies which were so small as to be invisible escaped through the closely-ranked teeth of these ivory rakes. Then with the end of the Second World War came the scourge of all fleas great and small. They called it D.D.T. It came in many shapes and forms from sprays and powders to creams and liquids. Overnight it annihilated hundreds of distinctive breeds of fleas.

They were the descendants of those which irritated Brian Boru before Clontarf and Napoleon after Waterloo. These were the same fleas whose ancestors ravished the soft white flesh of Eastern Europeans when Genghis Khan was a boy, the same that spread pernicious anaemia among the weaker and paler of the crowned heads of Europe when crowned heads were as plentiful as crows in a cornfield. It must be conceded that their contribution to the consistent and unmitigated scratching of the human body was greater than that of all other causes put together.

The other causes behind human scratching, itch, mange, assorted sores, hives, etcetera, were also thoroughly demoralised and utterly annihilated with the advent of sulpha and other powerful drugs in the years immediately after the Second World War. Imagine, therefore, my surprise on Sunday last when I beheld this relict from a flea-bedizened age as he sought relief from the tantalising itch which persecuted him. In my youth almost everybody in the congregation would indulge briefly or at length in a bout of scratching. While sinners and saints accumulated strength to combat temptation they also unwittingly accumulated bugs and fleas from those who sat alongside them during the hour-long ceremony of Mass and sermon.

Even the priests were tormented, as the Mass wore on by the unsolicited attentions of homeless fleas. During the sermon I would notice the most restrained of clerics squirm and cringe under the consistent assaults of these blood-crazed Siphonaptera, to invest them with their proper title. Unable to relieve himself the luckless sermoniser would raise his finger aloft to warn his listeners about some new form of evil. Cutely while his listeners eyes were glued to his wagging finger he gave himself a thorough scratching with the elbow of the same hand. It was that or abandon the sermon altogether. It was also proof of the old adage that quickness of the hand deceives the eye.

I have even seen bishops resort to these and other exceptional ploys while they held forth on the nature of the three divine persons or merely denounced the prevailing sanguine sins of the day. I recall a doughty, double-chinned canon whose body would tremble with rage while he castigated drunkards, seducers and calumniators to mention but a few of the ferocious wretches who scandalised the countryside at the time. At the height of his expostulations he would lift himself up by leaning his hands on the front of the pulpit. Here he would harangue for all his worth while his airborne feet, devoid of shoes, would scratch each other in places as diverse as ankle, knee, collop, back of knee, toe, thigh, heel and sole. All the time he maintained a resolute countenance, occasionally punctuated by momentary spasms of relief when a distressed area was comforted. Neither were businessmen above subterfuge when an unexpected itch or intransigent flea made scratching absolutely necessary. One of the best exponents of the shifty scratch I ever encountered was a county councillor who was often called upon to speak before the main event. He was a skilful enough orator, who never failed to draw applause with his witty sallies at the expense of the opposition.

It was when he was overwhelmed with the desire to scratch that he excelled himself. He would thrust a hand deep into his pocket and with the other hand point an accusing finger at a house in which dwelt a well-known member of the opposing party. There would follow a blistering attack on the character and motives of the accused. While all eyes were diverted the orator would furiously scratch himself with the trousered hand. Immediately he found relief the tirade would end until the desire to scratch returned once more. There are none of us free from the scratching urge. Stronger although less consistent than the sexual urge, there are times when the scratching urge simply cannot be denied. Diversion is necessary if one is under scrutiny and particularly if the area desirous of being scratched is one of the more private parts of the anatomy. Consequently I often feel deep concern for high-up people who must sit still during parades and other ceremonial occasions. To preserve an outward façade of placidity while the body screams out for itching is the very epitome of discipline.

There is nobody, be he bishop, general or president, immune from the desire to scratch. God alone does not scratch or if he does it must be his head with bewilderment at the behaviour of the world's inmates who daily seek to bring about their own destruction. This, however, is contemplative scratching and cannot be construed as legitimate or necessary scratching. The agony of the unscratched is no longer what it was. D.D.T. has seen to that. Up to this point I have made no mention of female scratchers. This is not intentional. I had intended all along to do so and it could be said in my favour that I was keeping the best wine till last.

I must say, however, at the outset that women are better able to conceal the desire to scratch than are males. This could be because it is not considered lady-like to scratch or rather was not considered so. Women's Lib would argue that they have as much right to scratch as men and I would hold firmly to this view.

Women are far subtler at scratching than are men. I remember a knitting party in a neighbour's house before the advent of D.D.T. It was a house renowned for fleas, not a terrible slur at the time since no house was without some number of the creatures. There was one outstanding scratcher in the group. There may have been others but this would never be revealed because most women who needed to scratch held out till they found themselves alone. Then would be the tearing and the scratching and the sighing with relief when they sunk long nails into the underscratched, long-suffering areas. They believed in the theory that one good comprehensive scratch was better than a hundred short-term, sneaky scratches. The restraining corset would be whipped off and cast aside while feverish fingers brought ease to the sore, sensitive flesh which had been mercilessly imprisoned for so long.

One of the knitting school was a professional scratcher. She never used her hands or fingers. She favoured the blunt instrument with which she knitted. When asked a question she would scratch some part of the anatomy as if she were visiting a reference book for the correct answer. She pretended to cogitate and contemplate while she scratched and scratched. There was no area of the body safe from the blunt head of the knitting needle and she never came up with the answer to the question until such time as every itchy area of the body was put thoroughly at ease.

I hope this short treatise on such a delicate subject will not set some of my readers on a course of scratching. Scratching is infectious and I, therefore, absolve myself from all responsibilty.

5 Cuckoo, Cuckoo!

> The Summertime is coming
> And the birds are sweetly singing

So runs the evergreen chorus. Summer's PRO, to wit
the bark-brown cuckoo, freshly arrived from Morocco,
has already made several pronouncements in places as
far apart as Knockanure and Newcastlewest. The gist
of his revelations is that the season is legitimately
under way now that he has established himself in a
ready-made nest, manufactured to measure by a brace
of innocent and well-meaning blackbirds whose off-
spring he simply heaved over the side to make way for
his ample African posterior. For thirty years or so
now, since I first started to write for money I have unfailingly made mention of the cuckoo's arrival.

I have published every report I ever received,
devoting lengthy paragraphs to the more meritorious.
Yet there are people who regularly come along and
ask me why I never write about the cuckoo. These
people know very well I write about the cuckoo. What
they are really asking is why I do not write about their
own special cuckoos or rather the individual cuckoo
which only they have heard. How true the old saying
that there is no cuckoo like your own cuckoo. On re-
flection I must honestly add that maybe there is no
such old saying. If this is so then I hereby sponsor it
for inclusion in the next anthology of old sayings.

By summer-time many of my readers will have heard a particular cuckoo. It is possible that substantial numbers may have heard the same cuckoo. If this is so console yourself with the fact that just as surely as no two cuckoos are alike so also are no two notes from any one cuckoo alike. The cuckoo's voice changes from day to day and fades away altogether after a few week's residence in his summer home.

Recently I read a distressing story concerning the decline in the numbers of cuckoos visiting this country during the summer. Despite the fact that the same applies to featherless visitors from America and England should not make our concern for the cuckoo any the less. While man multiplies all over the globe the number of birds, particularly cuckoos, tends to decrease. The chief reasons for this is that man requires more room and sacred retreats where cuckoos once advertised themselves are now housing estates and factories. I am not arguing against these. What I am trying to do is warn readers against a time when we will hear fewer and fewer cuckoos. A time will come when certain luckless individuals will wait in vain for that magical call which is part of the fabric of every summer. This is sure to give rise to shock and distress among the more susceptible of readers and it is only fair that they should be warned against the likelihood of summers without cuckoos. Personally I dread the thought but I have long since insured against it and I would strongly advise others that they should do the same.

In the event of cuckoo failure in the not-too-distant future we should be on the lookout for other signs of summer.

It takes a long time for summer to establish itself. For the first week or so it's no different from its predecessor. Gradually, however, it takes hold. More flowers appear and birds grow excited. The sting dies in the wind and all the cows are calved. There are many manifestations and each of us has his own special means of confirming that the season is well and truly launched.

For me summer comes with the arrival of a balding, sixty-year-old Clare man, a chap of roving eye and rosy cheek. For many years now he has presented himself at my bar counter at this precise time. He is as constant as the cuckoo or if you're that way inclined, the Northern Star.

On each visit he brings a female companion of far tenderer years than he. Yesterday which was Sunday he presented himself for inspection at 12.30 p.m. He had with him a stout lady who might have been twenty-five or thirty. He seated her and called for a drink. Two brandies with the barest tint of port wine in each if you please and where would we get a good lunch, not too exotic.

I shake hands with him and he introduces me to his girl of the moment. This is pure exhibitionism. He wants to show me what a randy womaniser he is. The girl smiles demurely, adjusts her buttocks on the seat and pulls an inadequate tweed skirt affectedly over fat red knees.

After this covert exercise our man winks lewdly at me as if to suggest that although a pornographic display had been publicly averted there was every likelihood of a comprehensive sexual debauch before the night grew pale and yielded to the dawn. Nobody believes this. Here is as prime an example of a frustrated cock virgin as one could wish to behold. I am reminded of *Titus Andronicus:* 'This is the monstrosity in love, lady, that the will is infinite and the execution confined,' which is merely another way of saying that bullocks' notions will avail you nought.

But let me describe this man who arrives unfailingly every summer. His chariot is an ancient Morris Minor. His women are invariably fat and serious-faced. His scant hair, dyed titian, is so cleverly combed that no part of the crown or poll of his head is without a diverting rib or two.

He has the best in false teeth upper and lower. Two biros and a fountain pen adorn his breast pocket. He belongs in another decade. You might say the man is dead but he won't lie down. He was weaned in dance-halls where paraffin lamps hung from the rafters and grated candles mixed with dance crystals glazed the uneven floor. Yet here he was publicly acknowledging the arrival of another summer.

His chances of courting a woman are slim, of carnally knowing a woman slimmer, of outright possession slimmest of all. Still he would subscribe to the Shakespearean theory, again to be found in *Titus Andronicus:*

> She is a woman, therefore may be woo'd;
> She is a woman, therefore may be won.

Outside in the street the people are coming from Mass. The fancies of boys and girls lightly turn to thoughts of love. The fat girl becomes restive. Her thoughts are far from love. A trickle of saliva emerges

29

from a corner of her mouth. Our man is pensive now, noting the other customers, particularly two good-looking girls who are seated opposite him. They are not, as yet, aware of his existence, yet he alone of all the people in the pub has paid his tribute to summer. Now that he has, however, he is mute. He has become a spent force. He is a smolt who will never again return to the clear and sparkling waters of the upriver reeds.

But he has accomplished his mission and this, for me, is the important thing. He has reminded me that it's high time I went into the kitchen and took the wife in my arms to tell her that summer is here and that love doesn't really change or grow grey. It's time to go some place, to get out and away into other places where we can be free for a while.

You can have your daffodils and your primroses. I don't begrudge them to you. Summer's representative has come from Clare. I return to the pub. I address him:

'You'll have a drink in honour of your visit.' His face lights up. Hope sparkles in his eyes. He nudges his girlfriend when I turn my back. His worth has been recognised. His day is made.

In acknowledging his visit I am also acknowledging or saluting the arrival of summer. I am making much of its representative, treating him with the courtesy and respect that I would normally reserve for accredited ambassadors.

6 Do You Like Cockles?

There is a relation of mine who is forever making promises he never fulfils. For instance he might say to me when mellowed by a few drinks, 'Do you like ducks?' I would, of course, answer in the affirmative. Straightaway he would promise me a brace of fat ducks which would never materialise. On other occasions he would enquire if I would be averse to a sack of turnips or cooking apples. 'Don't you dare buy a turnip,' he would say, 'for I have a pit of the finest only waiting to be boiled.' If it were apples he would advise us as to the best method of storing same. 'I'll bring enough,' he would say, 'to carry ye beyond St Patrick's Day.' Neither apples nor turnips would ever appear and there would be no mention of them when next the relation put in an appearance. It was as though he never made the promise. He would sit there pondering and admiring the contents of his glass and then suddenly he might ask, 'are you a man that likes floury spuds?'

I would reply that I like nothing better. He would savour the reply as though it were a rare cognac and eye me speculatively for a while before moving on to the next announcement.

'You wouldn't be put out,' he might say, 'if I was to land in here with a butt of spuds this day week?'

'No fear,' I would say.

'You'll like these,' he would go on, 'but I must warn

31

you to strain them the minute they're boiled or they'll burst into pieces and all you'll have is the skins.'

He had a slightly different if more dramatic approach towards my wife. Out of the blue he would say to her, 'Don't attempt to buy bacon next week.'

Immediately would follow a promise of a flitch of home-cured, streaky bacon. To give him his due he rarely promised the same commodity twice. I have lost count of the times he failed to deliver onions, cabbages, lettuces, beetroot, parsnips and carrots. His carrots, needless to mention, were redder and longer than any others as indeed were his parsnips white and thicker. His onions were as hard as golf balls while his lettuces were so succulent that no words could do them justice. To tell the truth I enjoyed his produce more than if I was actually presented with it. I would conjure up visions of steaming plates of streaky bacon and cabbage or multi-coloured, mouth-watering salads. He once gave me a description of a free-range chicken which he was specially nurturing so that I might have the benefit of the creature's natural broth.

'The minute he comes to the boil,' he told me, 'the flesh will drop away from the bones and you'll be faced with a shining white breast and two thighs that will melt in your mouth. The brown meat of the piobawn will come away like jelly and you'll need no teeth for the massacration of the heart, the kidney and the gizzard. The steam,' he continued as he placed a hand on my shoulder, 'off this fowl would be dinner enough for a weak sort of a man whilst the soup would bring a man ten days dead from his grave.'

No fowl anywhere could match up to this description but he would crown it all by concluding,

'You're sure you won't take it personal if I pluck and truss him for you?'

'Of course not,' I would reply.

'There's some that would you know,' he would confide. 'There's some odd people that cannot be satisfied.'

I would respond to this by declaring that it takes all kinds to make a world or some such inconsequential contribution. Time would pass but the free-range cockerel so nicely trussed and plucked would never arrive. I must confess that if it did I would have been deeply disappointed. He once promised me a young gander for Christmas. 'All I'll say,' he said as he squeezed my shoulder with one of his toil-hardened hands, 'is that you'll never eat another gander.'

What this meant was that no other fowl would ever match up to the one with which he would be presenting me. The whole business was quite harmless and my wife and I would listen with intent looks on our faces as he made promises that would never be fulfilled. The trouble arose when he struck up a conversation with someone who didn't know his form. This happened once a few weeks before Christmas. A new bank official had arrived in town a few days before and had brought his missus out for a drink or two in an effort to get to know the people of the area. Who should they meet on the occasion but my relation. Ever a decent man in a public house he insisted on buying a drink when he discovered they were strangers to the community. The drink borrowed another and soon the three were deep in earnest conversation.

A week was to pass before I was visited one morning by the bank official's wife.

'Has a parcel arrived for me?' she asked.

I responded in the negative and she said that she would call on the following day. This she duly did but no parcel had arrived. It was only then it dawned on me that my relation might have responsibility for the promised parcel. I asked her if this was the case and she confirmed that it was.

'What exactly did he promise you?' I asked.

'A turkey,' she replied, 'and a Christmas cake.'

'To be delivered here?' I prompted.

'Yes,' she replied.

'I'm afraid,' I told her, 'the turkey or the cake will never materialise.'

'But,' said she, 'he warned me not to buy a turkey for Christmas. He said he would deliver one here free of charge, trussed and plucked and ready for the pan. He said his wife and he were throwing turkeys out the door they had so many of them.'

'And the Christmas cake?' I prompted again.

'He told me his neighbour worked in a cake shop and that he would get him to bake a Christmas cake free of charge.'

'Did he promise you anything else?' I asked knowing only too well that he would never be content with such meagre promises so close to Christmas.

'Yes,' she said. 'He was to leave in a box of mixed vegetables and a sack of eating apples.'

I was, alas, obliged to disillusion the unfortunate woman. Luckily she had told me in time. Otherwise she might have had a bare board for the Yuletide. The next time my cousin called I took him to task. He genuinely had no recollection whatsoever of the banker's wife and expressed great regret that such inconvenience had been caused. I begged of him not to make any more rash promises to strangers, pointing out that it wasn't too bad as long as it was kept in the family. In fact I suggested that it might be time he abandoned these foolish promises altogether. He agreed with me completely and called for a drink. As soon as he finished it he called for another.

'Tell me,' he said as he sloshed the liquid around and around carelessly in his glass.

'Tell you what?' I asked.

'Do you like cockles?'

Absently I answered that I did.

'Very well,' he said, 'you'll have a five-gallon drum of cockles here under your nose on Saturday.'

So saying he finished his drink and went away. The cockles, of course, never appeared but the next time he arrived he had the good manners to ask me if I was partial to mussels.

Only the other day a man I have never seen before arrived and asked my wife if a side of smoked salmon had been left in our safekeeping for him. When she responded in the negative the man looked surprised. I have no doubt he'll call again and again before he eventually gets the message. It is hard to disbelieve this particular relation of mine when he gets into his stride. Maybe you have friends or relations like him. If you have don't discourage them. They'll always restore your appetite.

7 Unlicensed Bulls

Lately I met a small farmer who was summoned and
fined for possession of an unlicensed bull.

'You're an educated man,' he said to me, 'so maybe
you can tell me something.'

'I'm at your disposal,' I assured him.

'Does bulls take it to heart the way we does?' he
asked. What he meant was this. Is the sense of loss
experienced by the unlicensed bull who has been
apprehended by the bull inspector on a par with
human loss of the same kind? A hypothetical question
perhaps but one which deserves to be carefully considered nevertheless. The answer, of course, is that
there is a greater sense of loss because man has other
outlets for his pent-up energy. The bull is equipped for
one function and one function only and that is the
simple siring of cows and heifers. Imagine the sense of
deprivation felt by the unlicensed bull when the
meadows start to bloom and the yellow brilliance of
buttercups brightens the hills and valleys. Imagine the
indescribable frustration when giddy heifers scamper
by to a change of pasture on highways visible to the
incarcerated bull whose only role, now that he has
been found deficient by the Department, is to fatten
himself for the butcher's block.

Imagine the unutterable sense of unfulfilment when
a lone cow browsing the roadside grasses peers
through the hedge where the victim is confined. Their

eyes meet and for a long while they stand separated by the hedge contemplating what might have been. Then the cow, as is the wont of cows, resumes her grazing while the baffled bull bawls his heart out in desperation.

Small wonder that bulls have savage tempers. Nature is never easily thwarted but when it is agony replaces ecstasy. Does not even the stupefied bullock simulate the actions of his uncut brothers when he recalls his rightful function from the recesses of his clover-dimmed memory? Imagine then dear reader how much worse it is for the unlicensed bull possessed, I need hardly add, of all his faculties. He does not savour the perfumed hedgerows which surround him. To him these are the stiflers of his natural talents. Imagine his murderous wrath at the indignity which has been so unfairly forced upon him.

On the brambles small birds are chirping to each other their sweet notes of love while all around rabbits and hares are blissfully preoccupied with the age-old, delightful rites of propagation. Even the lowly insect drones out his love and is requited. Every creature of the field and thicket is free to pursue his lustful instincts without fear of being thwarted.

Alone of all these the unlicensed bull must suffer the humility of enforced loneliness while worse bulls with the departmental seal are allowing themselves to be petted and ogled by a superfluity of love-hungry heifers. I mentioned before how a friend of mine with a long neck for which defect the unlicensed bull is struck off, was free to marry twice and nobody objected. Let us return for a moment to this friend During the Emergency he joined the Irish army and was accepted without question.

They never even measured his neck when they allotted him his uniform. Nobody from corporal to major-general even once mentioned his neck during his lengthy service with the defence forces. Yet our friend the unlicensed bull who only wants to play the role of lover and father is denied these basic rights and consigned to a life of ineffectuality because of whimsical preferences which presently prevail in the Department of Agriculture.

A most interesting question arises from all this, of little consequence admittedly to those who are lacking in concern, and it is this: Which suffers most? Is it the bull who is whipped away when he has grown accustomed to the joys of love and the bliss of bovine companionship or is it the unfortunate virgin bull who has never experienced the ecstasies or satisfaction of cow and heifer-mating?

Certainly it must seem like a difficult question but those of us who are settled down in life will heartily concur with the viewpoint that a bull who has experienced the joys of love suffers most. There are those who will come down heavily in favour of the virgin bull but against this it must be submitted that what he has never had he will never miss. Others may argue that it is worse to be left in a permanent state of surmise and frustration, that all this leads to is a very befuddled bull fit for nothing but the humane killer but I would argue that the bull who has grown used to consistent copulation with cows and heifers suffers beyond all comprehension when he is ruthlessly cut off from his seemingly bottomless reservoir of romance.

The one true conclusion which we may draw from

all this is that unlicensed bulls, excepting those who are not apprehended, suffer more than their share in this world. The next time, therefore, you see a bull on his way to market during the early summer, ponder well his fate and thank your stars that those unjust laws do not apply to you or yours.

8 Twomey's Dog

I would like to deal now with a decent dog of a bygone
age, a dog whose services to his master deserve to be
recorded for posterity. He was an ancient Kerry Blue
who answered to the name of Bonzo. He was owned
by Michael Twomey, a prominent and benevolent
publican who once enjoyed a flourishing trade in the
street where I was born. Twomey's was the last
licensed outpost between the town of Listowel and the
north country which contained the villages of Knockanure, Tarbert and Moyvane. It was also a flour and
meal store and a great port of call for countrymen and
countrywomen alike. The women were permitted to
make their own tea in the kitchen while the men drank
stronger portions in the bar.

During Michael Twomey's tenure from the early
twenties to the late forties after-hours drinking was
commonplace in Listowel. Twomey's was no exception, a fact to which I can testify since I remember
in the early forties when we were daily threatened
with invasion this renowned public house was used as
a resting place for certain members of the Local
Defence Forces, that gallant and largely unsung body
of quiet men who rallied to the country's defence
when the call went forth.

My late father and his next-door neighbour were
members of a patrol which nightly investigated any
and all happenings on and about the old Mail Road

between Listowel and Tarbert. When the duty time of some of the patrol members ended they were fond of repairing to Twomey's where they might sip a hot whiskey or two and discuss the fortunes of the Allies and Axis who were at it, hammer and tongs, in north Africa. Fair play to the Civic Guards they worked in close liaison with the patrol and often exchanged notes as well as rounds in the snug warmth of Twomey's back kitchen in the early hours of the morning.

In short they looked with forgiving eyes at the numerous infringements of the licensing laws. Then the war ended and everything changed. Twomey's became a target for the occasional Sunday night visitation from patrolling members of the Garda Siochana. It was here, I am happy to say, that Twomey's Kerry Blue, the one and only Bonzo entered the picture. All night long he lay in what seemed to be the deepest of sleeps outside Twomey's front door. The knock of admittance to Twomey's at the time was two sharp raps on the fanlight with a coin. This pass-word never failed to gain admission. Inside there would be a black sugar bag folded around the electric light bulb to lessen the glare. It would take Virgil that great master of onomatopoeia to do justice to the contented, communal murmuring which was to be heard rising above the smoke-filled air in the warm public house atmosphere. There was extraordinary happiness here. All past tribulations and impending woes were temporarily forgotten while Twomey, bespectacled and benign behind the counter, stood ready to meet the wants of his chosen customers. Here was a sanctuary from domestic friction, from critics and creditors.

41

Then suddenly Twomey would raise his right hand high to attract attention. Gradually the hum of happy conversation would recede until absolute silence reigned supreme. All eyes and ears were on the alert as slowly and serenely the unmistakable and unearthly olagóning of the dog Bonzo came from the direction of the front door. It meant only one thing, that Civic Guards were on their nightly rounds and would be pausing shortly outside Twomey's to determine from patient listening, certain extra-sensory characteristics and other intuitions whether or not illegal trafficking in liquor was being conducted inside. Guards could easily deduce from vague sounds which meant nothing to other passers-by the number of drinkers hidden in the darkness of a premises and even the identities of the drinkers from various stifled groans, grunts and sighs.

The patrolling Guards of the time were not unlike visiting missioners of the same period. As with the preachers there would be a quiet Guard and a cross Guard. The quiet Guard would be for passing by but the cross Guard would have none of it. He would listen most assiduously for long periods and endeavour to peep through cracks or crevices to see what was happening inside. All the time the quiet or good Guard stood by with a look of embarrassment on his face. Shrewd judges insisted that it was an act which the Guards were fond of putting on to confuse curious watchers.

Inside there would be no sound of any kind and he who might wantonly break the silence would be banished from the premises for the remainder of his natural drinking life. Only those who have spent these

42

long silent periods in licensed premises after hours know how sailors trapped in a submarine feel. No one knows what is happening on the outside, whether relief is at hand or not. Minutes pass by like individual eternities. The air grows clammy. Worst of all every glass is empty and there is an unholy thirst which only the presence of danger can generate. Twomey would stand transfixed behind the counter like a setter waiting for the game to rise. There were brave souls driven to the point of suffocation with the desire to cough or at least clear a cloggy throat but no. They manfully held out till mercifully from outside came the prolonged high-pitched ululation of Twomey's Kerry Blue, the one and only Bonzo. It was a clear and resonant cry, persistent as any all-clear siren of the period. It was greeted by the trapped drinkers with prolonged cheers and mighty roars of relief.

'To Bonzo,' Twomey would call when every glass was filled.

'To Bonzo,' would come the unanimous response.

9   Bygone Barrel-Tappers

Now we will turn to an aspect of activity without which the supply of the nation's most popular drink, i.e. porter, might easily have been cut off during peak periods under the old licensing laws. I refer to the tapping of barrels, those cooper-made casks of wood banded with hoops of iron and filled with that luxurious black draught so beloved of country people and townspeople alike.

Often on certain nights there would be an overflow of business and the porter on tap would run out before its time. This necessitated the tapping of at least an extra half tierce. Busiest Sunday nights were those on which Duffy's and Fossett's circuses came to town. There was also excess business on the Sunday nights of football finals and generally on the sabbaths of July and August when the buck navvies were home on holiday from across the water. These had crowds of hangers-on and in those days they came home in great numbers to the delight of local bums and scroungers.

When the porter ran out there were many timorous publicans who called it a night and ordered their customers to evacuate themselves. Other publicans made hay while the sun shone. They had to. There would be bleak winter nights when customers were few and far between. During those days in the town of Listowel there was a certain Civic Guard who had a great ear for barrel music. That is to say he could hear a barrel being tapped at the other end of town. He could even tell the pub from where the sound of tapping was emanating. There were some who said he knew the individual tapping style of every publican in the town of Listowel and he would say to his companion on the beat, 'There goes so and so,' and with that he would take off towards the offending premises.

To counteract his keen ear certain precautions were necessary. In my case I would select a mature, able-bodied man with excellent eyesight and a thorough knowledge of the town's streets and back lanes. I would then roll in a half tierce and prepare my tap by binding it with old newspaper. I would then locate my mallet and measure up to my half tierce. On your wooden barrel of those days no two bungs were alike and great care had to be taken if the bung was not to be burst altogther.

As soon as I had taken thorough stock of the proportions of the half tierce I ordered my man on to the streets to see if all was clear. Our procedure was carefully prepared from long experience. As soon as he found himself outdoors he first looked up and down. Then he was gone like a flash on a tour of likely guard-paths. If all was clear he would return breathlessly to my front window and knuckle four noisome knocks thereon. That was the signal to tap. Up first with the barrel on the stand. In this chore I was aided and abetted by loyal friends whose wait for porter was soon to be at an end. If my man on the street gave only two knocks it meant that our friend with the ear for barrel music was too close for comfort and the tapping had to be postponed until he was at the maximum distance from the pub. When he hovered for too long in the vicinity the body of the tap and the bung area were covered with wet cloths in order to soften the sound. This greatly increased the chances of a burst bung and volunteers with gallons, basins and buckets stood by to capture the strong jets of high porter which always escaped when the tapping went wrong. Despite all the Sunday night activity it was seldom indeed that a publican was convicted. He would be raided regularly but so lax was the method of raiding that the patrons had no problem escaping the law. The law did not strain itself of course.

Biggest hypocrites of all in connection with the after-hours trade were successive governments who cheerfully accepted the taxes gathered by the publicans despite the fact that most of these taxes were collected after hours. Some whose salaries were partly paid out of this illegally-gathered money were frequently vociferous in their condemnation of publicans who indulged in after-hours trade. The political skulduggery still exists to a certain degree and I am always amused by politicians who condemn after-hours drinking but reap the big profits without as much as a blush.

Gone now are the great wooden barrels, the nickel and copper taps, the vent plugs, the mallets, the jugs and the basins and all the paraphernalia so necessary to the public house trade of the time. Gone too are most of the Civic Guards of that period. By and large they were a patient and understanding bunch of gentlemen and if a few were unsporting isn't there always a bad apple in every barrel. They were a great body of men and many is the brilliant game of cat and mouse we indulged in during the long nights of winter. I doubt if any of the customers of the time were possessed of motor cars so that there was no danger of car accidents. Neither had they enough money to get drunk.

This then constitutes a salute to the porter drinkers of a bygone period.

10 The Tumberawrd

Last week in one of Listowel's better-known backways I stood talking to a friend who regaled me with an account of an ingrown toenail which would shortly take him to hospital for an operation. I listened without any degree of concentration and indeed he seemed to sense this for in the middle of his narrative he excused himself and walked away. It was then I noticed a man watching me.

He was accompanied by a woman who clutched a handbag to her midriff and whose dentures tended to fall down about her lower lip thereby revealing a surprising expanse of pink gum. She wore a hat and she held a child of the female gender by the hand. The man wore a black overcoat and a white shirt open at the neck. As I passed by I tendered the entire party a very civil good morrow. In return the man, who struck me as a highly unsuccessful small farmer, did not acknowledge my salute.

Instead he stopped dead and looked me straight between the eyes. Then he uttered one word. The word was 'tumberawrd'.

I was taken completely by surprise because the word was a complete stranger to me. It was neither Irish nor English nor to the best of knowledge was it Latin, Greek or French. The man stood there waiting, while the woman transferred her handbag to a safer area under her oxter and instructed the child to blow its nose into an off-white handkerchief which had come out of her pocket.

'Tumberawrd,' I repeated in the hope that some additional words might be forthcoming. None were. The man just stood there with eyes that were filled with hope.

'Tumberawrd,' I said again. The man and woman nodded enthusiastically. In vain I searched my memory. I broke the word up into separate syllables and rejoined them but I was no nearer a solution.

I took a closer look at the man. He had dark eyes, a sallow complexion and greasy black hair. He looked like an Italian but how could he be an Italian, I asked myself? What would an Italian and his wife and child be doing in a Listowel backway? Then a thought struck me. Some months before while having a drink after a football match in one of Moyvane's livelier hostlries, I was informed by Batty Stacpoole that he suspected the presence of a papal spy in the area. At the time I tended to disbelieve Batty on the grounds that there were no heresies or schisms in the Moyvane district but now I wasn't so sure. Could this man be the papal spy in question?

At the time I had a few drinks inside me, after a surprise meeting with an old friend, and was somewhat susceptible to the ludicrous. Still the man was there and he had the appearance of a scattermouch. I decided to take no chances.

'Viva il Papa,' I said. The man shook his head.

'No,' he countered, ''tis the tumberawrd.'

This at least was a clue. The thing was an object of some kind. Preceded by the definite article the word was definitely not a salutation or message. The man was, therefore, not a papal spy.

'The tumberawrd,' I repeated after him.

He nodded happily. So did his wife and child. At last his question was to be answered.

However, the expectation died quickly on his face and he was about to move away. Suddenly a thought struck me. Could it be the title of a play and could this man possibly have identified me as a playwright of sorts and could he be seeking a copy of the play for reading or production purposes? It was a good title, 'The Tumberawrd'.

'How many acts in it?' I asked.

'There is not acts in it that I know of,' the man said.

'Then it's a book,' I suggested. He shook his head. At this stage the wife intervened.

'It's not a play or a book,' she explained, 'it's a tumberawrd.'

I digested the word once more. Tumberawrd. Tumberawrd. The Tumberawrd. For the life of me I could not make head nor tail of the thing. The man's wife was speaking again.

'The Tumberawrd,' she said. 'Jack McKenna's Tumberawrd.'

Here at last was a tangible clue. It was Jack McKenna's Tumberawrd. At once everything was clear. I smiled. The man smiled. His wife and child smiled.

'You want McKenna's timber yard,' I said.

'That's right,' said the man, 'the tumberawrd.'

I gave him his directions and he departed with a look of profound relief on his face.

Later than night I asked several intelligent people of my acquaintance if they could tell me what a tumberawrd was. One, a Civic Guard, told me it was a kind of tambourine, and another, a teacher, informed me that it was a kind of a harp.

No one gave me the right answer which would indicate none of us is as wise as he thinks.

11 Long Sermons

We will now turn aside from worldly matters and address ourselves to things ecclesiastical. Not by bread alone doth man live although you'll find few bakers to agree with such a sweeping statement. Indeed as shall be seen we are more indebted to wine.

Believe it or not I have no objection to long sermons in church. I always wake up from them feeling greatly refreshed. On the other hand, short, instructive sermons keep me awake and present no opportunities for dozing. The days of the long sermon, however, seem to have vanished forever. Consequently I was amazed last Sunday to hear a succession of faint, happy snores coming from the pew in front of me. The sermon was short and to the point so the snores could not possibly have been induced by boredom. Then came the unmistakable whiff of recently-consumed whiskey and all was made clear. The alcoholic fumes had blunted the sharpness of the poor fellow's wits and he had succumbed to slumber.

We once had a parish priest in Listowel, many moons ago, who specialised in long sermons. Oddly enough nobody objected. He had a soft voice which did not carry very far and since microphones had yet to be introduced to pulpits the majority of his listeners accustomed themselves to the sonorous drone of his preaching, folded their arms contentedly and drifted quietly into the land of half-sleep. These long sermons did them the world of good. At the conclusion they blinked happily into wakefulness and approached the rest of the Mass with revived interest. To them the long sermon was what half-time in a football game was to the tiring midfielder, a well-deserved lull, a chance to recharge the batteries so as to be able to participate fully in what might lie ahead. This is not to say that they missed out on the spiritual benefits of the sermon. Far from it. Always, between nods, they managed to grasp the gist and the gist is what really matters. I remember once to have been seated near an uncle of mine who was renowned for dozing in church especially during yearly Retreats. Fair play to him he never drifted off altogether. As soon as the sermon began he would allow his noble head to sink between his shoulders, his paunch to extend itself comfortably in front of him and his folded hands to rest contritely thereon as if he were settling himself to devote all his attention to the oncoming homily. On his face would appear a look of consummate bliss mixed with genuine piety.

On the occasion in question the sermon had to do with marital infidelity. It lasted for three quarters of an hour. Afterwards when we were outside under a sky which was filled with sinless stars I asked him what he thought of the effort.

'All that poor man was trying to say,' said he, 'is that forbidden fruit is to blame for many a bad jam.'

Here was the gist of the entire forty-five minutes sermon. He had absorbed the full text through his subconscious and rendered it down to a phrase as pithy as one could wish to hear. He was unmarried, of course, and as an addendum to his summary he said: 'If you had less marriages you'd have less of that kind of thing.'

To return briefly to the drunken snorer of Sunday last he too, I must say, is becoming the exception rather than the rule. I remember a time not too far distant when the back of the church sounded as though it had been assailed by a massive swarm of bees such was the volume of the muted snoring and deep breathing in that area. Largely this would be caused by gentlemen who like to drink their stout and whiskey before Mass. There were, of course, sober sermon-snorers who slipped the moorings of consciousness the moment the preacher appeared in the pulpit. His arrival was the signal for which they had waited since entering the church. In short when he opened his mouth they closed their eyes. These homiletic slumberers were never in fear of attack from the pulpit since it was impossible to deduce whether their eyes were closed in concentration or in self-induced insensibility. Even those wakeful souls who sat beside them had no way of knowing. Personally speaking I am a man who finds it difficult to keep my eyes open during a long sermon or indeed during a long anything. You'll never succeed in convincing me that a long sermon is better than a short one. You would be more profitably employed convincing a man dying from sunstroke that the earth is really ninety-three million miles from the sun.

12   Voracious Visitors

Last week we had seven rounds of visitors none of whom had any real claim on our hospitality. They came, they saw and they ate. Then they vamoosed. Let me give a few words of advice to those readers who may fall foul of these touring vultures whose sole aim is the exploitation of those they visit.

There was a relation of ours, a withdrawn, unpretentious poor fellow who would arrive in town unfailingly for the second day of Listowel Races. He would park his bicycle in our backyard, remove the clips from his trousers, comb his hair and politely refuse the offer of tea which had been made to him. When the offer was repeated he might say: 'Alright so. I'll take a cup out of my hand.'

This was to imply that he did not wish to inconvenience anybody, that he was utilising the minimum amount of ware, foregoing the use of a saucer and even of a chair where he might, if he were less considerate, roost for the day and be an encumbrance to everybody. The trouble with these models of self-effacement was that they looked upon the drinking of tea as a form of diversion rather than a means of sustenance. What a cup out of the hand meant in conventional terms was that the recipient recognised the need for some form of communication between himself and his relations but being retiring and bashful could do no more than 'take tay' with them. The trouble was that he never knew when to take his leave and would often stand quietly for hours on end clutching his cup as though it were his only lifeline with the immediate world around him.

The most dangerous type of visitor is he who when invited to partake of a cup of tea announces firmly that he has only just risen from the table. Very good if he presents himself with this fable at a time other than meal time but if he arrives while a meal is in progress be certain that, if given a second invitation, he will eat the unfortunate host out of house and home. This has always been my experience with the man who has just risen from the table. To be fair to him, however, he has more or less laid his cards on the table which he now faces. He does not say: 'I am already sated, having partaken of a meal a few moments ago.' He does not say, 'I could not look at a bit.' He simply says: 'I'm only just after rising from the table.' Inherent, however, in this seemingly conclusive pronouncement is a warning for those who will heed it. The warning might well be worded like this: 'I am truly after only rising from the table but this does not preclude me from sitting at another table if pressed to do so.'

Watch out, therefore, for men who say they have just risen from the table for these are creatures of gluttonous and rapacious natures who cannot and will not make do with the produce of one table and who are forever on the lookout for invitations to partake of the produce of other tables.

Most sinister of all visitors and very often the most misleading is he who sits himself down and waits to be asked if he will partake of a cup of tea or a snack but who, when accepting the offer, does so conditionally.

'I will,' says he, 'if ye'er all having it.' The implication here is that he does not consider himself a worthy enough guest to merit a meal or part of a meal on his own and so he suggests that unless there is a meal in the offing as a matter of course he will not accept. This is what he would like to infer but very often, alas his message becomes garbled in transit and is quite often taken to mean this: 'I will accept your kind offer to dine but only on condition that everybody else dines as well.' This display of magnanimity endeared him at once to those in attendance who were not regular members of the household and even if his suggestion was enacted it was not those who provided the repast who were praised for their generosity and why should they be praised! Were it not for the conditional clause contained in the acceptance of the visitor there would have been nothing for anybody. Was it not logical, therefore, to give thanks to him rather than to the householder?

There were many houses where, because of abuses of the aforementioned nature, the householders were reluctant to be expansive when offering refreshment to visitors. 'Sure you won't have tea?' was a common safeguard employed by those who had been bitten too often in the past. What this meant was that the house holder was more than willing to lay the table for tea but the visitor had given the distinct impression that he was already overfed and in no need of tea. It could also mean this: 'You can have tea if you like and all that goes with it but I'm sure you are far too busy and important a man to be bothered with tea.'

Another suitable ploy is to stir up the fire until the flames induce the kettle to start singing. This should provoke the visitor into asking the following question: 'I hope you're not boiling that kettle for me?' Thus a tea-making situation is averted because he has implied that he does not wish the kettle to be boiled, especially for him. He may, of course, if pressed allow the kettle to be boiled for him but the tendency in this less hospitable day and age is not to provide tea unless it is specifically asked for. There was a time in this much-abused land when there would be a mad rush to rinse out the teapot the moment a visitor was sighted on the roadway.

I hope our findings on this occasion will be of some assistance to those who have suffered more than their share from voracious visitors who depend largely on excursions to liberal households for their daily bread.

13 Phenomena

My personal definition of a phenomenon is something which cannot be properly explained, something not unlike myself. Reputable dictionaries have different meanings for the word. One says that a phenomenon is something which is exceedingly remarkable. The *Oxford Dictionary* more or less agrees but goes one better when it says that a phenomenon is a thing that appears or is perceived especially a thing, the cause of which is in question. I can hardly be blamed, therefore, if I stick to my own definition but decide for yourself whether the events set out in the following paragraphs are truly phenomena or are they commonplace incidents not worth recording. I am convinced too that phenomena are like bills. When you get one others are sure to follow and no matter what precautions one takes one is never fully prepared for them.

These supernatural happenings began on Monday afternoon as I took my leave of the busy streets and byways of my native town and directed myself in the general direction of the rain-freshened, hail-dotted countryside. There was a sting in the air so I wisely decided to call at a wayside inn before entirely abandoning myself to the rigours and alarums of the wilderness. I called and paid for a glass of whiskey. I was about to indulge in a preliminary sip when an insignificant bald-headed gentleman tugged at my sleeve and intimated coyly that he would like to join me. I allowed him to dangle at the end of my elbow for a moment or two while I considered his request. He was, from his appearance, a man of the roads, itinerant to some, tinker or traveller to others. A solitary nasal dewdrop hung precariously at the end of his puce-coloured, pock-marked proboscis. A practised cough racked his frame. It left him shuddering and shivering. From all outward appearances he looked like a man at the end of his tether.

I bought him a half glass of Irish whiskey and laid upon him a blessing of good health. He drank the whiskey and demanded a pint of stout. When I pointed out to him that the government of this country had consistently failed to provide me with the funds to purchase drinks for the man on the street he scoffed and spoke as follows:

'If I warn't a tinker,' he said, 'you'd soon stand to me.'

'But,' said I, 'you're bald and the world knows that there is no such creature as a bald-headed tinker.' I quoted for him a passage from the ruminations of the late Jack Faulkner whose pronounciamentos on itinerant matters are the next thing to infallibility. I told him how Frank Hall in his earlier television programmes had conducted a highly successful nationwide search for a bald-headed tinker.

'But I am sir,' he said. 'I am a tinker.'

A tear appeared in his eye and I could see that he was telling the truth. I bought him the pint and left the premises having first finished my whiskey. The countryside at once opened its arms to me. I moved happily along congratulating myself on having stopped for the drink. If I had not stopped I would not have encountered the phenomenon of a bald-headed tinker. The second phenomenon followed almost immediately. A pony and cart guided by a bogman of my acquaintance passed me by at a modest trot. I saluted the driver who responded, albeit slurrily, with a weatherly comment. In the body of the car sat two tiers of peat briquettes containing in all a dozen bales of this excellent factory-produced fuel. This was the second phenomenon. Here was a man from the heart of a first-class bog bringing, as it were, coals to Newcastle. At home the fellow was surrounded by black, glinting turf-banks begging to be cut yet here he was paying good money and undertaking a return journey of several miles for that which he already had in abundance at home if he only took the trouble. Surely this was something which defies analysis and this is what phenomena are all about.

No doubt whatsoever my star was in the ascendancy. How fortunate I was to have witnessed two phenomena in a row and all in a matter of minutes. Two thoughts occured to me. Would my readers believe me when they read of them? Secondly, had I really witnessed phenomena?

Marvelling at these exciting manifestations of the extraordinary I continued upon my way until I reached a narrow byroad which also happens to be the main thoroughfare through the biggest, most under-developed bog in the area. This bog is a favourite haunt of mine, a great place for contemplation or for putting together handy lines of dialogue as the mood catches one. I sauntered in the general direction of a setting sun blissfully alone with my thoughts. Suddenly there was a rumble and a roar behind me and I jumped to one side in order to allow an oil lorry to pass by. The roadway wobbled and sagged under the weight. Water seeped from its soggy supports like cider from a press. For a while it seemed that this ancient causeway must collapse. But no. It steadied itself, shook itself free of the last remaining drops and stretched evenly before me as though it had never entertained such a monstrosity.

Here surely I told myself is the ultimate phenomenon, fuel from Arabia being transported to the home of fuel, all the way by pipelines, tankers, terminals and trucks at tremendous expense to a spot where the finest fuel in the world could be had for nothing. Conveyed over oceans and continents at the risk of life and limb this greasy, smelly produce of the middle-east was supplanting the aromatic peat of our fathers and forefathers. This surely was the final sell-out to the horrific conglomeration known as progress. The lorry stopped at a small house which was surrounded by rich boglands as far as the eye could see. The driver alighted from his cab and injected a thick tube into a tank that stood at the rear of the house. This, I told myself, could happen nowhere but in the land of holy wells, in the island of saints and scholars. There should be, I told myself, a television camera present to capture forever this priceless moment of Celtic madness.

14   The Council of Dirha

> Good luck and success
> To the Council of Trent,
> What put fast upon mate
> But not upon drink.
>
> *(Overheard at a wake)*

When the above couplet was conceived there was fasting on Fridays. Nowadays, Lent apart, we may eat meat with impunity throughout the entire year. The Church was quite clear in its strictures regarding the consumption of meat and meat products on days of fast and abstinence. Then in 1966 Pope Paul promulgated new laws for Roman Catholics. Fast days which had included all the weekdays of Lent, the vigils of Pentecost, the Immaculate Conception and Christmas and the Ember Days were reduced to two, i.e. Ash Wednesday and Good Friday. In the same decree Pope Paul reaffirmed the laws of abstinence from meat. However, he allowed episcopal conferences to substitute for abstinence with other forms of penance, especially works of charity and exercises of piety.

Hobside theologians of the time were known to smirk at the expression 'works of charity'. They deduced in their own indigenous fashion that to be charitable one had to be rich. Since neither they themselves nor their associates were remotely connected with wealth, they regarded themselves as being incapable of charity. When it was explained to them that charity had other connotations such as love of one's fellow man they were quick to point out that because of their innate worthlessness no one, save their own family, placed any value on their love.

However, this is another matter. It is with the pre-Pope Paul period of fast and abstinence that I propose to deal now. Before I do let me say that fireside theology was reduced to a very fine art in those days. There was no opposition from television and the country was also far from being motorised. Consequently there was genuine profundity in most fireside exchanges. The subtler arts of sarcasm, irony and cynicism all flourished and were brought to such a degree of excellence by common country folk that ordinary comment was almost totally outlawed.

The first serious council held by hobside theologians to which I was witness was held in Dirha Bog circa 1935. So great was the fear of excommunication in those distant days that even today I am not at liberty to mention the name of the house owner. The council was well attended and present at the time were such venerable sages as the late Sonny Canavan and Jack Duggan. The main spokesman, however, was a *spailpín* by the name of Billy Drury, a brother of the poet, Paddy. The main item on the agenda on that memorable occasion was whether the consumption of blackpuddings on a Friday constituted a breach of the laws on fast and abstinence. Porksteak and puddings were a common enough diet at the time. Every countryman kept his own pig and when the creature was fat enough to be butchered substantial quantities of pork steak and home-filled blackpuddings were distributed among the neighbours.

It was universally accepted even amongst the most extreme heretics and schismatics that under no circumstances was the eating of porksteak to be countenanced on Fridays or on any other days of fast and abstinence. Puddings, however, were a different kettle of fish altogether. If I might be permitted to the use of a widely-used saying of the time, 'there were puddings and puddings'. It was with this aspect of the matter that the Dirha theologians concerned themselves. When is a black pudding not a black pudding or, to put it another way, what are the chief characteristics of a sinful pudding?

Billy Drury opened the proceedings with a story explaining at the outset that it was to be taken in lieu of his conclusions on the subject in question. I now propose to exploit the Drury paradigm to its fullest.

Some years earlier he had worked with a farmer to the north of Listowel. In a croteen at the lee of the house there was a prime pig fattening. When the time was ripe one of the children of the house was dispatched to the house of the local pig butcher. Duly the pig was killed and butchered, the meat salted and barrelled, the porksteak cut away and the blood readied for the filling of the puddings. This last chore was always undertaken by the woman of the house. Eventually all the puddings were filled, boiled and placed in tall tiers so that they might cool. When they were sufficiently cooled the man of the house, without a word to anybody, produced a frying pan, greased it with lard and placed it on the red hot Stanley range which dominated the kitchen. He then went to the tiers of pudding and withdrew a substantial ring for himself.

'Will you sample one of these?' he asked Drury.

'I'm your man,' Drury responded. The man of the house placed both puddings on the pan where they immediately set up a sibilant sizzling. This was followed by a heavenly smell as the puddings started to cook. Both men sat happily by the range while the fat spat and the puddings crackled. Then came the unexpected. Down from the bedroom in her long flowing nightdress came the woman of the house. First she looked at the pair by the range and then she looked at the pan.

'Do ye know,' she said with a sting to her voice, 'the day we have?'

When neither answered her she pointed out that is was Friday and that if either one partook of the puddings he would be risking eternal damnation. Both men shuffled uneasily in their seats. The man of the house rose but Drury stayed put. The man of the house preceded his woman to the bedroom casting a cold look at the frying pan and an even colder one at Drury. To make a long story short, Drury consumed both puddings in their entirety.

The hobside theologians digested the Drury story and cogitated upon its many implications while they filled or relighted their pipes. Finally a man from Affoulia spoke up.

'You committed a mortal sin,' he said, 'and that's the long and short of it.'

Others disagreed and for a while the argument ranged back and forth. It was Drury however who had the last word.

'I was a witness,' said he, 'to the filling of the puddings. The blood was salted. Common oatmeal and massecrated onions was all that was added. If a sin was

66

committed then it was a venial one and a very watery venial at that. If,' Drury continued, 'the puddings was filled by the likes of Mary Flaherty and if I was after guzzling two of them then it would be a mortal sin for Mary Flaherty's puddings is stuffed with every known groodle from spice to pinhead oatmeal.'

At this stage there were murmurs of approval from the council. Mary Flaherty's puddings were known and prized from the Cashen river to Carrickkerry.

Drury was quick to press home his point. He listed the numerous ingredients of the Flaherty puddings from the chopped liver of the pig itself to the minutely gartered gristle. He pointed out that the two puddings which he had eaten on the Friday at the farmer's house were not legitimate puddings and by no stretch of the imagination could they expect to qualify as whole or legal puddings under the act. Drury went on to state that one of Mary Flaherty's puddings was a meal in itself and thereby contributed to the breaking of the law laid down by the Council of Trent.

The council re-lighted its pipes and cleared its throats. In the end it held that Drury had done no wrong. Had the puddings in question been up to the Flaherty standard there would be no doubting his guilt. The puddings were inferior, therefore incapable of contributing to a sinful situation.

The conclusions of the Council of Dirha were accepted locally until 1966 when Pope Paul's promulgations changed everything.

15   The Inflammable Blackpudding

Did I ever tell you about the blackpudding that caught fire when its texture was tested by matchfire in my public house after hours. I should perhaps mention that the manufacturer of these puddings was a man greatly addicted to strong drink. As a result the quality of the puddings was inconsistent. He was a liberal-hearted fellow in addition to being an out-and-out drunkard. His poison was a shot of Irish whiskey chased by a bottle of three-to-six month old stout. Into every batch of puddings he poured a bottle or two of poitín. On this particular occasion there was no poitín so he used a quart of methylated spirits. The result was that this particular batch of puddings was highly inflammable. All the other batches were first class and frequently he would invite customers to have a look at the pudding-making process favoured by him. His door was never closed. It was his way of showing that he had nothing to conceal, that only the best went into his puddings.

I once called to his premises. He was covered in blood at the time. He happened to be mixing the contents of a new batch. He indicated a case of bottled stout which lay under the table. I uncorked two bottles and handed him one. From the back pocket of his blood-saturated trousers he withdrew a flat bottle of poitín and offered me a swig. It was pretty potent and a long way from being mature. He took a swig himself and chased it with a long swallow of the bottle stout. I gave him a hand filling the puddings. The skins were ready and it was no bother to stuff the mixture of blood, suet, onions and stale bread into the waiting cortexes and a simpler matter to transfer them to a cauldron of water which was simmering away cosily on a nearby Stanley number nine. Every so often he would stir the blood with a stout blackthorn stick he held ready for such a purpose. That would be the sloshing and the swishing as the rich, red mixture swirled in the pot.

When all the puddings were in the cauldron he poked the range fire with an iron poker and very soon there was a gurgling and a chortling as the blood-red, surface bubbles indicated that the water had begun to boil. He withdrew the puddings expertly on the butt of a fishing rod, ringing each one with consummate skill until there was room for no more on the butt. He placed the buttful to one side and continued with the withdrawal. When he had finished he took a jack-knife from his back pocket and cut one of the steaming puddings in two. He handed me one half and at once set to devouring the other half himself. I must say that they were highly palatable although to my mind they still needed a bit of refining in a frying pan.

That particular pudding-maker has long since departed the worldly scene. The harsh diet of bottled stout, poitín and unfried puddings took their toll and he succumbed to a variety of internal maladies before his time. Like the nursery rhyme his puddings were subject to two extremes:

> When they were good they were very, very good
> When they were bad they were horrid.

Let us now look back upon that memorable night when his produce was the cause of such a colossal conflagration. Let me set the scene. The pub was filled with a mixture of local tipplers and part-time alcoholics from the rustic hinterland. A black sugar bag shrouded the electric light bulb already dappled with moth and bee droppings. Muted whispers were the only sounds permissable. Outside there were two members of the Garda Siochana on public house duty and none of us knew when they would smite upon the pub door and utter that terrible phrase which has paralysed publicans for generations: 'Guards on public house duty.' It was a happy gathering. The porter flowed freely as the hours passed quietly and serenely without conflict or dissension.

As the hour of midnight approached most of the customers invested in a ring or two of blackpudding and the half of a tile loaf. In those halcyon times the cost of this substantial if controversial repast was a mere shilling or in today's worthless coin a five-penny piece. I often recall the contented sound of that bygone grinding and chewing, a tribute surely to the man who filled the puddings.

There they were, my customers, masticating away to their hearts' content, sighing now and then with that deep satisfaction which only lovers and pudding-grinders can dispense so eloquently when all of a sudden a normally quiet-spoken chap, one Moses O'Day, jumped to his feet and committed the unpardonable sin of raising his voice in a public house after hours. 'There is something wrong with my pudding,' he shouted. Those who sat nearby endeavoured to subdue him. They assured him that the

70

puddings were no different from the batches consumed on other Sunday nights. He wouldn't hear of it. He committed the second sin of the night when he produced a box of matches and cracked one. The sound erupted out of the pub silence like the discharge crack of a point twenty-two. This was followed by a flaring and a flickering likely to alert every Civic Guard in the town. Before anyone had the wit to stop him he held the match close to the pudding in order to inspect its texture.

What happened next is history. There was a bright orange flash followed by a ferocious whoosh. In a fraction of a second the pudding was consumed by the hungry flame and all that remained in our friend's hand was a black cinder, the mortal remains of a once-plump blackpudding. There was nothing for it but to clear the pub at once before the Guards came to investigate. In a few moments there was nobody left on the premises.

As things turned out the Civic Guards never came but later that night I examined a solitary blackpudding which remained unpurchased on the counter after all had gone. I put a match to it and it took fire at once, wriggling for a moment as though it were alive before it too was consumed utterly by the flame. It was later we learned that instead of the usual pint of poitín the quart of meths had been added to the pudding mixture.

A few weeks later while bent over his blood bath the pudding maker slumped forward and fell head first into the pudding mix. He had just consumed nine bottles of stout and a half pint of poitín. He managed to extricate himself from the mess and rushed into the street. When he saw his image in a shop window he screamed like a man demented. A doctor was summoned and as soon

71

as it was discovered that pudding blood and pudding blood alone was the cause of his delirium he was immediately hosed down and escorted home. He never filled a pudding thereafter which is a pity because his puddings were powerful as well as palatable and were always a delight to behold.

16 Buying a Goose

Before Christmas I successfully engaged two geese. If you're ever taken down in the purchase of a goose, that is to say if you buy an old goose instead of a green one, you will not engage geese hastily nor will you buy at random from any Tom, Dick or Harry. To be quite candid I would put the same amount of preparation and planning into the purchase of a goose as I would into the robbing of a bank. Too many times in the past I was taken down in the matter of geese by otherwise honest people. In the country it is not considered a dishonest act to sell old geese to townies. Old geese must be sold to somebody and who better than townies. Few townies know the identities or dwelling places of goose producers so the disposer is nearly always safe from retaliation. In addtion nearly all goose producers look alike, especially those who foist off ancient birds on the unwary and the unsuspecting.

You will always find them in the corner of the market where the ass and pony rails are thickest and they will always call you 'Sir' which, in my humble estimation, is the true hallmark of a scoundrel.

Luckily for me I have considerable experience in the engaging of geese. At the tender age of thirteen I was dispatched to the marketplace in Listowel having been commissioned to invest in a prime goose by an elderly neighbour. It was foolishly presumed at the time that I was a crafty young chap who would be more than a match for the wiles of dealers anxious to dispose of old geese.

Earlier that morning I was instructed in the ways of geese. Old geese were listless. Their eyes were lack lustre. Their beaks were more worn and of a darker yellow than those of young geese. Their laipeens were wrinkled and coarse. These were but a few of the many characteristics attached to geese and ganders of advanced years which were conveyed to me that morning by the pair who commissioned me to transact the purchase.

Armed with this vast array of knowledge and clutching two florins in my trouser pocket I entered the market. Great was the clamour of geese and turkeys not to mention ducks and drakes and hens and chickens. Ass and pony rails cluttered the scene. Everywhere bargains were being struck and satisfied customers departing with cross-winged braces of prime fowl grasped in either hand. I hardly knew where to begin. I looked in wonder at the great array of transports and countryfolk.

'Ah,' said a friendly voice behind me, 'is that yourself.' I barely recognised the visage of the man who addressed me. I knew him and yet I didn't know him. He had a friendly face, the sort you could immediately trust. He knew my name although I couldn't tell his.

'I bet I know what you're looking for,' he said. 'I bet you're after a turkey for your mother.'

'No,' I said, 'I'm after a goose for oul' Mague Sullivan.'

'If you are,' said he, 'you'd better draw away from here,' and he winked in the most conspiratorial way possible. I followed him past rails of gobbling turkeys, madly quacking ducks and hissing ganders. 'Half of these,' my new-found friend announced indicating the proprietors of the fowl all about us, 'would pick the eye out of your head or,' said he in a whisper, 'if you was gom enough to stick out your tongue that's the very last you'd see of it.'

He stopped at a corner of the market where an old shawled woman with a wrinkled face was attending to an ass-rail of geese. She had, I recall to this very day, the kindliest and homeliest face one could wish to see. Her voice was soft and sweet and as near to Gaelic in sound and rhythm as English could be. More to the point she had geese for sale. My friend explained my predicament, how my purchasing power was restricted to four shillings and how I had been warned about dishonest people who would think nothing of fobbing off an elderly goose on an innocent person.

'Oh, *mo creach agus no leir,*' said the old woman to the heavens, 'may God in his mercy preserve us all, the young as well as the old, from them that would wrong innocent people.'

She made the sign of the cross after this aspiration and went, as she said herself, for to capture the tenderest goose in her rail.

'This is a fine sensible fellow here,' said she lifting up a chesty specimen for my approval.

'I declare to God,' said my friend, 'but that's as noble a young gander as I seen in sixty years, man and boy. Pay down your money quick, don't let someone else come and sweep him on you.'

I could not find the four shillings quickly enough. I handed it over and was given in return the bird which had so recently been exhibited. Proudly I hurried back to the house of Mague Sullivan.

'*M'anam an diabhal,*' said she when she beheld the gander, 'he's like he'd be the one age with myself.' She called her husband and between them they set up a terrible lamentation. There were nothing for it but to return to the market, recover my four shillings and re-invest in a younger goose.

In the market I returned to the same corner but there was no sign of the old woman. I searched each of the three other corners in turn and when these failed I went from ass-rail to ass-rail. The bother was that nearly every old woman wore a shawl and each of their faces was as wrinkled as the next. Each was also politer than the next when I addressed them. Anyone of a dozen of them could have been the woman from whom I had purchased the venerable gander.

17 Success with Women

or How to Succeed with Women

There was, in Ballybunion, when I was a youth a tall, slinky slow-foxtrotter who was frequently forced to fight off women whenever a ladies' choice was announced. Remember that I speak of a time when good foxtrotters were as plentiful as pismires at a picnic, when the strains of Pat Crowley's music brought out the best in otherwise uninspired terpsichoreans, when there were cups for quick-steps and waltzes and dance halls were really for dancing. Our slinky slow-foxtrotter did not stand out on the ballroom floor. There were no flourishes to his finishes and I never once saw him execute a really neat combination of steps.

He was a careless dresser. His shortcoat was never buttoned and his trousers were never pressed. Neither was his hair racked nor his shoes polished. When I was in my heyday a man never combed his hair. He racked it or if you like raked it. In country places in those days a comb was called a hair rake.

The rest of us went to great pains to polish our shoes and maintain knife-edge creases in our trousers. We plastered our hair with tuppenny bottles of superfine brilliantine and we always topped our cigarettes and buttoned our shortcoats before inviting a lady to dance.

Our friend was different. I had better put a name on

him although readers who were part of the Ballybunion
scene in those halcyon times will have him tagged from
the opening line. He was known as Bango Malone. He
was not, strictly speaking, a native of Ballybunion. He
spent most of the summer there with an aunt and he
came from the Tralee side which could mean anywhere
between Tarbert and Ballinskelligs. He had a season
ticket for the Pavilion ballroom but little else by way of
worldly matters. He is now deceased as is the aunt who
provided his long summer holidays.

He was an easy-going chap, no more than twenty but
he had about him an air of quiet assurance which belied
his tender years. We envied him. No woman ever
refused a dance and as I have earlier pointed out he was
besieged before the drums rolled for the start of a
ladies' choice. Sometimes a damsel with exceptional
looks would appear in the Pavilion. When she showed
no inclination to accept the countless offers to dance
made by some aspiring foxtrotters like myself we
looked to Bango to see if he could make any fist of her.
There was no need to worry. After a while he would
sidle in her general direction and before he was half
way to her she would be on her feet waiting for him to
sweep her into his arms.

What was it about him we asked ourselves? He was
nondescript enough. He never used superfine
brilliantine as we did. He never cracked jokes and the
women he chose as partners never laughed during the
period of the dance. He wasn't good at quips but he was
a consistent and slinkyslow-foxtrotter and this was the
only apparent asset of which he could boast.

Oddly enough we didn't envy him. He was never
smug and never in the least boastful about his

accomplishments in the female field. He never went home alone from a dance. There would be a rush for partners as Joe McGinty announced that the last dance of the night was at hand. The best looking girls were swept up quickly or rather they allowed themselves to be swept up by those they had earlier chosen to look after compacts or purses. Bango moved late. Joe McGinty would be singing the opening lines of *Goodbye Sweetheart* when he would drift across the floor to the lady of his choice. She would have refused earlier invitations and gambled all that Bango would select her for the ultimate caper. We marvelled at the ease with which he charmed every make of woman. He never spoke during that drowsy last dance. He held her close but not too close. She would endeavour to look into his eyes as if searching for a secret truth which might reveal the inner thoughts of his heart. Then and only then would he permit himself the very faintest fraction of a smile. As the magical melody wore on and Joe McGinty's sleepy sonorousness drugged us into dreamland Bango would be seen to be dancing cheek to cheek. When a lady consented to dance cheek to cheek it meant, without question, that she had allowed herself the luxury of an escort to her place of abode or mode of transport. Bango never asked. It just happened. With the rest of us it was different. Only on rare occasions could we induce a lady to leave the hall with us. Occasionally a kind-hearted soul would answer in the affirmative when permission was requested to see her home but for the most part we would be given one of the standard answers such as 'my sister is with me,' or 'my brother is waiting for me at the door.'

Another favourite rejection was for a girl to say she

had a cold and was afraid to pass it on. Others had to leave immediately after the dance while more went home in bevvies having been forewarned by anxious mothers to spurn would-be escorts and seek safety in numbers. Hard to blame the mothers for, beyond doubt, there were some unscrupulous rogues at large in Ballybunion at the time. It was the confluence of all romantics, lawful and unlawful for that place and period.

All this, however, does not help us in our analysis of Bango Malone. Bango is, of course, a *leas-ainm* or nickname. His real name was Beneficus or Benidicus or some such cumbersome attachment. His friends abbreviated this to Bango. There was none of us at the time who could explain Bango's success with the fair sex. Some, the more impressionable, took to imitating his mannerisms few and all though they were. We gave up using superfine brilliantine and tried not to be raucous or noisy as had been our wont. We let the creases escape from our trousers and gave up buttoning our shortcoats before asking a girl to dance. It was all to no avail. If anything we were less successful than before. It was as if the girls knew we were imitators because they refused to take us seriously. With Bango it was the same as always. At the end of their week's or fortnight's holidaying females would go home, heartbroken after Bango. He would promise to write but this alas was something he was incapable of doing having abandoned school at an early book.

Looking back now over the years it is not too difficult to understand his success with women. He never stood out like a sore thumb. He was never noisy. He never did anything brilliant while dancing yet he never did

anything foolish. He stayed away from the centre of the
ballroom. He was a headlands-dancer preferring to do
his eurhythmics in the quieter areas. I'll grant you there
are women who love the limelight, who like the centre
of the floor, who like to be in the thick of things
whether these situations are embarrassing or not but
the truth is that the vast majority of women are content
to go through life with the Bangoes of this world.

Bango succeeded because he was an average man.
He never lost because he never gambled. He never
made his partner look awkward on the dance floor. He
took no chances. He never bored her with idle talk. He
let the music and the atmosphere do the work and was
happy and which is more important was seen to be
happy whenever his partner searched for the truth in
his eyes. He wasn't great but neither was he mediocre.
Women sensed that here was a man who could go
through life without rocking the boat and this basically
is the chief requirement of a female in the long term.

If he were in the cavalry Bango would never lead a
charge. The chances were he'd live to tell the tale. He
knew his limitations. He wore his clothes the way he
did because he did not want to attract too much
attention. He could not cope with it if it came his way.
It was Shakespeare who said that 'the apparel oft
proclaims the man'. In Bango's case it was true. He
was, in short, a man who could lay a spell upon all
females great and small.

18   Tales for a Wet Day

'I'd like to go to funerals but I'm too small.' The remark was passed by none other than my friend Kevin McCarthy of Derrindaffe, Duagh. Derrindaffe is a mixed countryside containing some of the most verdant acres in north Kerry and some intense bush and bogland which needs reclaiming the way Ben Gunn needed a haircut. Kevin McCarthy was, you will have gathered, a small man and he maintains that his presence at funerals avails him little because of his size. In short nobody sees him. This, of course, is what attending funerals is all about. There are shy souls who are either unable or unwilling to sympathise with the next of kin as is the normal practice. It is, therefore, essential that they be seen. In this respect small, shy men like Kevin McCarthy are placed at an extreme disadvantage.

'If you had a bugle or a whistle,' said the *bodhrán*-maker Davy Gunn who happened to be in the company, 'you could let go a blast of your own choosing to let the relations know you were there.'

'A whistle I might,' Kevin concurred, 'but a bugle never, for might not our friend in the coffin think it was Gabriel's horn and go for getting up.'

All who were listening agreed with this pronouncement by the Derrindaffe man. It was two thirty of a Thursday afternoon. Outside a cold wind nattered and spluttered and a flight of pernickety hailstones beat an Arctic tattoo on the window panes. It was no day to be out of doors. A lone seagull drifted down the grey sky and a man from Carrigkerry in order to register his disapproval of the weather loudly blew his nose. A pair of independent farmers from the Ballylongford side entered and called for two hot whiskies.

'Ye're wise,' Davy Gunn told them, 'the day is fit for nothing else.' It was true for Davy Gunn. Apart from the downing of hot whiskies this particular Thursday was one which made for indoor recreations. In other words it was a time for the release of carefully thought-out observations. It was a time for the telling of yarns and tall tales. It was a time when countrymen come into their own. The setting was right for by now the wind had grown stronger and was more heavily laden with northern undertones. The hail had stopped but if there is anything more inconsistent than hail I would like to know about it. Hail comes and goes as does nothing else. Snow may fall all day and rain all night but hail is here one minute and gone the next. Its descent is sudden and murderous, its departure immediate and mute as though it had never been there at all. Perhaps its make-up is the fault of its brief tenure or perhaps it is the first passionate onslaught which is so momentary unlike snow which can drift in isolated flakes for hours before finally falling for days on end or rain which may precede itself with mysterious mists for long periods. Hailstone has no overture but all this is getting us nowhere so let us return to the cosy interior of the pub where our yarn spinners are gathered.

Kevin McCarthy may be too small for funerals but he

has a wide-ranging imagination which is a great asset in a public house.

'Apples,' said Davy Gunn, 'are gone stone mad. I'm after paying twenty-seven pence for those few.' He indicated a bag which contained a handful of undersized cooking apples. Apart from their smallness they were mottled, warped and otherwise mis-shapen.

'God be with the days,' said Davy Gunn, 'when you'd buy a ten stone sack of cooking apples for ten bob.' He sipped from his stout glass and went on to tell us an amazing tale. It appears his coarse brush was once swept away by a flood. He was a young chap at the time and, of course, had neglected to properly survey the lie of the land before parking the brush in the first place. There was nothing for it but to hasten to the nearby town of Listowel and buy a replacement. Money was scarce at the time and if coarse brushes were cheap itself they commanded the best part of a day's wages. Between the jigs and the reels Davy Gunn purchased the brush and returned home with it. No sooner had he put it into use than the head fell off and landed itself into a gutter which, at the time, was playing host to a modest flow of water. From the gutter the head of the brush floated into a nearby stream which was in excellent fettle waterwise after a prolonged period of heavy rain. Before Davy had time to recover the brush-head it had resigned itself to the current of the stream. In seconds it disappeared under a bower of overhanging sallies where the waters chuckled and boiled. From this turbulent spot it was carried directly to the Smearla river which bore it swiftly to the Feale river which in turn swept it downriver and deposited it on the grassy inch of a small farm near the village of Ballyduff.

Disgusted, Davy thrust the handle into the soft earth at the side of the byre which he had been endeavouring to sweep clean. There was nothing for it but to hit for town for another brush. However the rain fell all that afternoon so that he was forced to postpone the visit. In the end he was obliged to buy a new coarse brush for the simple reason that he had forgotten where he had thrust the handle of the old one. Time passed and spring turned into summer.

'I declare to God,' said Davy, 'I was sweeping alongside of the byre when I noticed the brush handle. There was blossoms on it so I left it where it was. By autumn the blossoms turned into apples.'

'Cooking or eating?,' Kevin McCarthy asked.

'Cooking,' Davy answered. The two farmers from Ballylongford exchanged looks and ordered a second pair of hot whiskies.

'That apple tree,' Davy went on, 'kept us in apples for twenty-five years until it bore no more fruit.'

'What happened?' asked Kevin McCarthy.

'I declare to God,' said Davy, 'but didn't it turn back into a brush handle again.'

The story was absorbed silently but respectfully. All eyes were now turned on Kevin McCarthy. That worthy coolly finished his glass of stout and called for another.

'When I was going to Derrindaffe National School,' Kevin opened, 'fruit was very scarce. You would seldom see blackcurrants or gooseberries although blackberries were to be had galore, in the fall of the year. The briar scairts would be black with them but somehow people hadn't meas-my-dog in them. Myself was the same. I would sooner the gooseberry or blackcurrant. Anyways this Pakistani came to the school one day selling penny pencils. Not many had a penny but I was one of those that had. I bought the pencil and when I went home that night I put the pencil into use but devil the scrawl could I get it to make. I'd be better employed with a thorn or a *cipín* from an ass-rail.'

At this stage Kevin took a swallow from his glass. There was silence for awhile. All knew the story was not quite finished.

'I threw that pencil out the window and it landed in the middle of the haggard,' Kevin went on, 'and it bloomed into the finest gooseberry bush you ever saw.'

'Eating or cooking?' Davy Gunn asked.

'Eating,' Kevin answered at once.

'And did it turn back into a pencil?' the chief of the two Ballylongford farmers asked.

'Indeed it did nothing of the kind,' Kevin told him. ''Tis as healthy as you or me or Davy Gunn there and it bears fruit every summer that brings the branches to one level with the ground.'

'Of course anything would grow in Derrindaffe,' Davy Gunn corroborated.

'A gooseberry bush without gooseberries is of no use to anyone.' This observation was made by a rangy man from the Athea direction.

'Birds might want it,' Davy Gunn interposed.

'Oh yes of course,' the Athea man agreed, 'there is that.'

'A gooseberry bush without gooseberries,' said Kevin McCarthy, 'is like a suit of clothes with no money in the pockets.'

This was well received and if those present were in the habit of applauding you may be sure that Kevin McCarthy would have received a mighty accolade.

'What happened the lead?' the Athea man wanted to know.

'What lead?' asked Davy Gunn.

'The lead in the pencil,' the Athea man answered.

'What happened to the lead in all our pencils?' Davy Gunn enquired by way of conclusion.

MORE BOOKS BY JOHN B. KEANE

Letters of a Successful T.D.
Letters of an Irish Minister of State
Letters of an Irish Parish Priest
Letters of an Irish Publican
Letters of a Matchmaker
Letters of a Love-Hungry Farmer
Letters of a Country Postman
Letters of a Civic Guard
Unlawful Sex and other Testy Matters
The Gentle Art of Matchmaking
Is the Holy Ghost Really a Kerryman?
Death Be Not Proud and other stories
Strong Tea
Self Portrait